BETTY PARASKEVAS

ILLUSTRATED BY

Michael Paraskevas

Harcourt Brace & Company

SAN DIEGO   NEW YORK   LONDON

Requests for permission to make copies of any part of
the work should be mailed to: Permissions Department,
Harcourt Brace & Company, 6277 Sea Harbor Drive,
Orlando, Florida 32887-6777.

Library of Congress Cataloging-in-Publication Data
Paraskevas, Betty.
Monster Beach/written by Betty Paraskevas; illustrated
by Michael Paraskevas.—1st ed.
p.   cm.
Summary: a rhyming story about a young boy who is
frightened by a mysterious sea monster while visiting
his grandfather's beach house.
ISBN 0-15-292882-0
[1. Sea Monsters—Fiction. 2. Seashore—Fiction.
3. Grandfathers—Fiction. 4. Stories in rhyme.]
I. Paraskevas, Michael, 1961–   ill. II. Title.
PZ8.3.P162Mo   1995
[E]—dc20   93-46927

PRINTED IN SINGAPORE

First edition
A B C D E

The paintings in this book were done in acrylics on canvas.
The display type was hand-lettered by the illustrator.
The text type was set in ITC Berkeley Oldstyle Medium.
Color separations were made by Bright Arts, Ltd., Singapore.
Printed by Tien Wah Press, Singapore
This book was printed with soya-based inks on Leykam recycled
paper, which contains more than 20 percent postconsumer waste
and has a total recycled content of at least 50 percent.
Production supervision by Warren Wallerstein and Kent MacElwee
Designed by Michael Farmer

To Jerry Della Femina—
East Hampton's very own charismatic sea monster

To Jesse Weisfelner—
For his faith in the virtue of sea monsters

—B. P. and M. P.

GRANDFATHER AND I decided to stay
At our fishing shack while my folks were away.
We arrived at night and crossed the dune
By the ghostly light of the silvery moon.
I saw something crack the glassy sea
And rise in the water ahead of me.

I turned and made a beeline back
To the safety of the fishing shack.
I locked the door and never said
A single word but went straight to bed.

We rose with the sun, and I began to feel
Foolish as I carried my rod and reel
Across the dune. It was very clear
My eyes had played tricks. There was nothing to fear.

I'd been fishing for an hour alone on the shore
When the thing I'd seen the night before
Just beyond the breakers, raised its head.
And I saw those eyes, flaming red.

I turned and ran across the sand,
Clutching the fishing pole still in my hand.
When I turned again and looked to where
That monster had been—he wasn't there.

I decided not to say a word;
The whole thing sounded too absurd.
Then the lifeguard arrived, and very soon
The umbrella brigade was crossing the dune.

I watched the umbrellas around me bloom.
When Grandfather arrived there was barely room
To plant *his* umbrella and unfold his chair.
The beach was crowded, and I was aware
Of scolding parents and the constant noise
Of cranky little girls and boys.

Three naughty boys who looked the same
Were kicking up sand, playing a game.
The sight of the triplets always struck fear
In the hearts of the folks who vacationed each year
In the cottages surrounding our fishing shack—
But in spite of our prayers, they'd always come back.
And every summer as those triplets grew,
Their devilish pranks got more devilish, too.

Suddenly they grabbed an old man's hat
And sent it out to sea with a baseball bat.
The old man jumped right out of his seat,
Shaking his fist and stamping his feet.
Mad as he was, he chased the three.
They escaped by swimming straight out to sea.

We heard the lifeguard's whistle screech—
He signaled the triplets back to the beach.
They were excellent swimmers and chose to ignore
The shrill command. We watched from the shore.

All at once the sky turned gray,
And the sea turned from blue to green.
The ocean was wild and the waves were so high
The triplets were not to be seen.

The lifeguard rallied some of the men
To help launch the lifeboat. Again and again
It was tossed back to shore by a cascading wall
Of salty seawater that drenched them all.

Then we saw the sea monster with his ridiculous grin
Struggling to bring the triplets in.
They clung to his back; it was touch and go,
As he fought the powerful undertow.
Time after time he failed as he tried
To reach the beach against the tide.

Then he rose up high on one huge wave,
Still carrying the three he was trying to save.
He slid to the beach and collapsed in a heap,
And all the children began to weep
As the monster, still with the old man's hat,
Breathed one last sigh and went completely flat.

The children wept softly, and the triplets, of course,
Wept the hardest of all. They were filled with remorse.
Grandfather said he'd be right back,
And made a quick trip to the fishing shack.

Everyone watched as he gently applied
A tire patch to the monster's side.
Then he pumped him up there on the shore,
Till he looked exactly as he had before.

The wind died down and the sun came out.
People shook hands and danced about.
The sky turned from gray to blue
And when it did, the sea did, too.
We sat around that afternoon
And sang "By the light of the silvery moon."
The triplets were angels; all the children behaved.
The grown-ups were friendly; the monster was saved.

From that day on the legend grew,
About Monster Beach, where the sky is more blue,
Where the sand and sea sparkle, and just off the shore
Lives a lovable monster all the people adore,
Who brought us together and taught us to care,
With respect for each other, in a place we all share.